ALSO BY COLM TÓIBÍN

The
Testament
of
Mary

COLM TÓIBÍN

SCRIBNER

New York   London   Toronto   Sydney   New Delhi

Scribner
A Division of Simon & Schuster, Inc.
1230 Avenue of the Americas
New York, NY 10020

Originally published in 2012 in Great Britain by Viking Penguin

First Scribner hardcover edition November 2012

Designed by Carla Jayne Jones

Manufactured in the United States of America

3   5   7   9   10   8   6   4   2

Library of Congress Control Number: 2012007578

ISBN 978-1-4516-8838-2
ISBN 978-1-4516-9075-0 (ebook)

Some of this novel was used as the basis for the play "Testament," performed
at the Dublin Theatre Festival in October 2011.

For Loughlin Deegan and Denis Looby

The
Testament
of
Mary

They appear more often now, both of them, and on every visit they seem more impatient with me and with the world. There is something hungry and rough in them, a brutality boiling in their blood, which I have seen before and can smell as an animal that is being hunted can smell. But I am not being hunted now. Not anymore. I am being cared for, and questioned softly, and watched. They think that I do not know the elaborate nature of their desires. But nothing escapes me now except sleep. Sleep escapes me. Maybe I am too old to sleep. Or there is nothing further to be gained from sleep. Maybe I do not need to dream, or need to rest. Maybe my eyes know that soon they will be closed for ever. I will stay awake if I have to. I will come down these stairs as the dawn breaks, as the dawn insinuates its rays of light into this room. I have my own reasons to watch and wait. Before the final rest comes this long awakening. And it is enough for me to know that it will end.

They think I do not understand what is slowly growing in the world; they think I do not see the point of their questions and do not notice the cruel shadow of exasperation that comes hooded in their faces or hidden in their voices when I say something vague or foolish, something which leads us nowhere. When I seem not to remember what they think I must remember. They are too locked into their vast and insatiable needs and

1

too dulled by the remnants of a terror we all felt then to have noticed that I remember everything. Memory fills my body as much as blood and bones.

I like it that they feed me and pay for my clothes and protect me. And in return I will do for them what I can, but no more than that. Just as I cannot breathe the breath of another or help the heart of someone else to beat or their bones not to weaken or their flesh not to shrivel, I cannot say more than I can say. And I know how deeply this disturbs them and it would make me smile, this earnest need for foolish anecdotes or sharp, simple patterns in the story of what happened to us all, except that I have forgotten how to smile. I have no further need for smiling. Just as I had no further need for tears. There was a time when I thought that I had, in fact, no tears left, that I had used up my store of tears, but I am lucky that foolish thoughts like this never linger, are quickly replaced by what is true. There are always tears if you need them enough. It is the body that makes tears. I no longer need tears and that should be a relief, but I do not seek relief, merely solitude and some grim satisfaction which comes from the certainty that I will not say anything that is not true.

Of the two men who come, one was there with us until the end. There were moments then when he was soft, ready to hold me and comfort me as he is ready now to scowl impatiently when the story I tell him does not stretch to whatever limits he has ordained. Yet I can see signs of that softness still and there are times when the glow in his eyes returns before he sighs and goes back to his work, writing out the letters one by one that make words he knows I cannot read, which recount what happened on the hill and the days before and the days that fol-

THE TESTAMENT OF MARY

lowed. I have asked him to read the words aloud to me but he will not. I know that he has written of things that neither he saw nor I saw. I know that he has also given shape to what I lived through and he witnessed, and that he has made sure that these words will matter, that they will be listened to.

I remember too much; I am like the air on a calm day as it holds itself still, letting nothing escape. As the world holds its breath, I keep memory in.

So when I told him about the rabbits I was not telling him something that I had half forgotten and merely remembered because of his insistent presence. The details of what I told him were with me all the years in the same way as my hands or my arms were with me. On that day, the day he wanted details of, the day he wanted me to go over and over for him, in the middle of everything that was confused, in the middle of all the terror and shrieking and the crying out, a man came close to me who had a cage with a huge angry bird trapped in it, the bird all sharp beak and indignant gaze; the wings could not stretch to their full width and this confinement seemed to make the bird frustrated and angry. It should have been flying, hunting, swooping on its prey.

The man also carried a bag, which I gradually learned was almost half full of live rabbits, little bundles of fierce and terrorized energy. And during those hours on that hill, during the hours that went more slowly than any other hours, he plucked the rabbits one by one from the sack and edged them into the barely opened cage. The bird went for some part of their soft underbelly first, opening the rabbit up until its guts spilled out, and then of course its eyes. It is easy to talk about this now because it was a mild distraction from what was really going on, and it is easy to talk about it too because it made no sense. The bird did not seem to be hungry, although perhaps it suffered from a deep hunger that even the live flesh of writhing rabbits could not satisfy. The cage became half full of half-dead, wholly uneaten rabbits exuding strange squealing sounds. Twitching with old bursts of life. And the man's face was all bright with energy, there was a glow from him, as he looked at the cage and then at the scene around him, almost smiling with dark delight, the sack not yet empty.

By that time we had spoken of other things, including the men who played with dice close to where the crosses were; they played for his clothes and other possessions, or for no special reason. One of these men I feared as much as the strangler who arrived later. This first man was the one among all those who came and went during the day who was most alert to me, most menacing, the one who seemed most likely to want to know where I would go when it was over, the one most likely to be sent to bring me back. This man who followed me with his eyes seemed to work for the group of men with horses, who sometimes appeared to be watching from the side. If anyone knows what happened that day and why, then it is this man who played with dice. It might be easier if I said that he comes in dreams but he does not, nor does he haunt me as other things, or other faces, haunt me. He was there, that is all I have to say about him, and he watched me and he knew me, and if now, after all these years, he were to arrive at this door with his eyes narrowed against the light and his sandy-coloured hair gone grey and his hands still too big for his body, and his air of knowledge and self-possession and calm, controlling cruelty, and with the strangler grinning viciously behind him, I would not be surprised. But I would not last long in their company. Just as my two friends who visit are looking for my voice, my witness, this man who played dice, and the strangler, or others like them, must be looking for my silence. I will know them if they come and it should hardly matter now, since the days left are few, but I remain, in my waking time, desperately afraid of them.

Compared to them, the man with the rabbits and the hawk was oddly harmless; he was cruel, but uselessly so. His urges were easy to satisfy. Nobody paid any attention to him except me, and I did because I, perhaps alone of those who were there, paid attention to every single thing that moved in case I might be able to find someone among those men with whom I could plead. And also so that I could know what they might want from us when it was over, and more than anything else so that I could distract myself, even for a single second, from the fierce catastrophe of what was happening.

They have no interest in my fear and the fear all those around me felt, the sense that there were men waiting who had been told to round us up too when we sought to move away, that there seemed no possibility that we would not be held.

The second one who comes has a different way of making his presence felt. There is nothing gentle about him. He is impatient, bored and in control of things. He writes too, but with greater speed than the other, frowning, nodding in approval at his own words. He is easy to irritate. I can annoy him just by moving across the room to fetch a dish. It is hard to resist the temptation sometimes to speak to him although I know that my very voice fills him with suspicion, or something close to disgust. But he, like his colleague, must listen to me, that is what he is here for. He has no choice.

I told him before he departed that all my life when I have seen more than two men together I have seen foolishness and I have seen cruelty, but it is foolishness that I have noticed first. He was waiting for me to tell him something else and he sat opposite me, his patience slowly ebbing away, as I refused to return to the subject of his desires: the day our son was lost and how we found him and what was said. I cannot say the name, it will not come, something will break in me if I say the name. So we call him "him," "my son," "our son," "the one who was here," "your friend," "the one you are interested in." Maybe before I die I will say the name or manage on one of those nights to whisper it but I do not think so.

He gathered around him, I said, a group of misfits, who were only children like himself, or men without fathers, or men who could not look a woman in the eye. Men who were seen smiling to themselves, or who had grown old when they were still young. Not one of you was normal, I said, and I watched him push his plate of half-eaten food towards me as though he were a child in a tantrum. Yes, misfits, I said. My son gathered misfits, although he himself, despite everything, was not a misfit, he could have done anything, he could have been quiet even, he had that capacity also, the one that is the rarest, he could have spent time alone with ease, he could look at a woman as though she were his equal, and he was grateful, good-mannered, intelligent. And he used all of it, I said, so he could lead a group of men who trusted him from place to place. I have no time for misfits, I said, but if you put two of you together you will get not only foolishness and the usual cruelty but you will also get a desperate need for something else. Gather together misfits, I said, pushing the plate back towards him, and you will get anything at all—fearlessness, ambition, anything—and before it dissolves or it grows, it will lead to what I saw and what I live with now.

Farina my neighbour leaves things for me. And sometimes I pay her. At first I did not answer the door when she knocked and even when I collected whatever she left for me—fruit, or bread, or eggs, or water—I saw no reason to speak to her as I passed her door later, or even pretend that I knew who she was. And I was careful not to touch the water she left. I walked to the well to get my own water, even if it left my arms strained and sore.

When my visitors came they asked me who she was and I was glad to be able to tell them that I did not know, and had no interest in finding out, and did not know either why she left things for me other than that it gave her an excuse to hover in a place where she was not wanted. I must be careful, they said to me, and it was not hard to reply, to say that I knew that better than they knew it, and that if they had come to give me unnecessary advice, perhaps they should think of staying away.

Slowly, however, as I passed her house and saw her at the door I began to look at her and I liked her. It made a difference that she was small, or smaller than I am, or weaker-looking even though she is younger. I presumed at first that she was alone and I believed that I would be able to deal with her if she became difficult or too persistent. But she is not alone. I have found that out. Her husband lies in bed and he cannot move and she must attend to him all day; he is in a darkened room. And her sons, like all the sons, have gone to the city to find better work, or more useful idleness, or some adventure or other, leaving Farina the goats to tend and terraces of olive trees to watch over and water to carry each day. I have made clear to her that her sons, if they ever should come here, cannot cross this threshold. I have made clear to her that I do not want their help for anything. I do not want them in this house. It takes me weeks to eradicate the stench of men from these rooms so that I can breathe air again that is not fouled by them.

I began to nod my head when I saw her. Still I did not look at her, although I knew that she would notice the change. And out of it came more change. It was difficult at first because I could not understand her easily and she seemed to think that strange but it never stopped her talking. Soon, I began to follow most of her words, or enough of them, and I learned where it was she went every day and why she went there. I did not go with her because I wanted to. I went because my visitors, the men who come to oversee my final years, had outstayed their welcome and asked too many questions and I thought that if I disappeared on them, even for an hour or two, they might learn greater civility, or, even better, they might go.

I did not think that the cursed shadow of what had happened would ever lift. It came like something in my heart that pumped darkness through me at the same rate as it pumped blood. Or it was my companion, my strange friend who woke me in the night and again in the morning and who stayed close all day. It was a heaviness in me that often became a weight which I could not carry. It eased sometimes but it never lifted.

I went to the Temple with Farina for no reason. And as soon as we set out I was already enjoying the thought of the discussion when I came back about where I had been, and I was already working out what I would say to my visitors. We did not speak on the way and it was only when we were close that Farina said that each time she went there she asked only for three things—that her husband be taken by the gods into death before he suffered more and that her sons be kept in good health and that they might be kind to her. Do you really want the first, I asked? Your husband to die? No, she said, I do not, but it would be for the best. And it was her face, the expression on her face, a sort of light in her eyes, a kindness as we entered the Temple, that I remember.

And then I remember turning and seeing the statue of Artemis for the first time; in that second, as I stared at it, the statue was radiating abidance and bounty, fertility and grace, and beauty maybe, even beauty. And it inspired me for a moment; my own shadows fled to talk to the lovely shadows of the Temple. They left me for some minutes as though in light. The poison was not in my heart. I gazed at the statue of the old goddess, she who has seen more than I have and suffered more because she has lived more. I breathed hard to say that I had accepted the shadows, the weight, the grim presence that came to me that day when I saw my son tied up and bloody and when I heard him cry out and when I thought that nothing worse could happen until hours went by. I was wrong to think that nothing worse could happen, and everything I did to stop it failed, and everything I did in order not to think about it failed too, until it filled me with its sound, until the very menace of those hours entered my body, and I walked back from the Temple with that menace still pumping through my heart.

With the money I had saved I bought from one of the silversmiths a small statue of the goddess who lifted my spirits. And I hid it away. But it meant something knowing that it was in the house close to me and I could whisper to it in the night if I needed to. I could tell it the story of what happened and how I came here. I could talk about the great restlessness that came when the new coins began to appear and the new decrees and the new words for things. People, both men and women who had nothing, began to talk about Jerusalem as though it were across the valley instead of two or three days' journey, and when it became clear that the young men could go there, anyone who could write, or was a carpenter, or could make wheels or work with metal, anyone indeed who could speak clearly, anyone who wanted to trade in cloth, or in grain, or fruit, or oil, they would all go there. It was suddenly easy to go there, but it was not easy, of course, to come back. They sent messages and coins and cloth, they sent news of themselves but whatever was there held them with its pull, the pull of money, the pull of the future. I had never heard anyone talk about the future until then unless it was tomorrow they spoke of or a feast they attended each year. But not some time to come in which all would be different and all would be better. Such an idea swept through villages like a dry hot wind at that time, and it carried away anyone who was any use, and it carried away my son, and I was not surprised by that because if he had not gone he might have stood out in the village, and people might have wondered why he did not go. It was simple really—he could not have stayed. I asked him nothing; I knew that he would easily find work and I knew he would send what the others who had gone before him sent, just as I wrapped for him what he would need as the other mothers did whose sons were leaving. It was hardly sad. It was simply the end of something, and there was a crowd when he left because that day others were leaving too, and I came home almost smiling at the thought that I was lucky that he was well enough to go and smiling too at the idea that we had been careful in the months—maybe in the whole year—before he left, not to talk too much or grow too close because we both knew that he would go.

But I should have paid more attention to that time before he left, to who came to the house, to what was discussed at my table. It was not shyness or reticence that made me spend my time in the kitchen when those I did not know came, it was boredom. Something about the earnestness of those young men repelled me, sent me into the kitchen, or the garden; something of their awkward hunger, or the sense that there was something missing in each one of them, made me want to serve the food, or water, or whatever, and then disappear before I had heard a single word of what they were talking about. They were often silent at first, uneasy, needy, and then the talk was too loud; there were too many of them talking at the same time, or even worse, when my son would insist on silence and begin to address them as though they were a crowd, his voice all false, and his tone all stilted, and I could not bear to hear him, it was like something grinding and it set my teeth on edge, and I often found myself walking the dusty lanes with a basket as though I needed bread, or visiting a neighbour who did not need visitors in the hope that when I returned the young men would have dispersed or that he would have stopped speaking. Alone with me when they had left he was easier, gentler, like a vessel from whom stale water had been poured out, and maybe in that time talking he was cleansed of whatever it was that had been agitating him, and then when night fell he was filled again with clear spring water which came from solitude, or sleep, or even silence and work.

All my life I have loved the Sabbath. The best time was when my son was eight or nine, old enough to relish doing what was right without being told, old enough to remain quiet when the house was quiet. I loved preparing things in advance, making sure that the house was clean, beginning two days before the Sabbath with the washing and dusting and then the day before preparing the food and making sure that there was enough drinking water. I loved the stillness of the morning, my husband and I speaking in whispers, going to my son's bedroom to be with him, to hold his hand and hush him if he spoke too loudly, of if he forgot that this was not an ordinary day. The Sabbath mornings in our house in those years were placid mornings, hours when stillness and ease prevailed, when we looked inside ourselves and remained almost indifferent to the noise the world made or the stamp the previous days had left on us.

I loved watching my husband and my son walking together to the Temple, and I loved waiting behind to pray before setting out to the Temple alone, not speaking, looking at no one.

I loved some of the prayers and the words read from the book aloud to us. I knew them and they came to mean soft comfort to me as I set out to walk home having listened to them. What was strange then was that in those few hours before sundown a sort of quiet battle went on within me between the after-sound of the prayers, the peace of the day, the dull noiseless ease of things and something dark and disturbed, the sense each week which passed was time lost that could not be recovered and a sense of something else I could not name that had lurked between the words of the book as though in waiting like hunters, or trappers, or a hand that was ready to wield the scythe at harvest time. The idea that time was moving, the idea that so much of the world remained mysterious, unsettled me. But I accepted it as an inevitable aspect of a day spent looking inward. I was glad nonetheless when the shadows melted into darkness at sundown and we could talk again and I could work in the kitchen and think once more of the others and of the world outside.

They move things when they come, my two visitors, as though this house were theirs, as though re-arranging the furniture will lend them a power in this room that nothing else can lend them. And when I tell them to put things back—move the table back against the wall, move the jugs for water from the floor onto the shelf where I normally keep them—they look at each other and then at me, making clear that they will do nothing I say, that they will wield power in the smallest ways, that they will give in to no one. When I look back at them I hope they see contempt or some reflection of their idiocy, even though I do not feel contempt, I feel almost happy and I feel amused at how like small boys they are in their random search for ways of showing who is the biggest, who is in command. I do not care how the furniture here is arranged, they can move it daily and it will not offend me, and thus I often go quickly back to my chores as though I have meekly accepted a defeat. And then I wait.

There is one chair in this room in which no one has ever sat. Perhaps in the past the chair was in daily use somewhere, but it came through this door during a time when I needed desperately to remember some years when I knew love. It was to be left unused. It belongs to memory, it belongs to a man who will not return, whose body is dust but who once held sway in the world. He will not come back. I keep the chair in the room because he will not come back. I do not need to keep food for him, or water, or a place in my bed, or whatever news I could gather that might interest him. I keep the chair empty. It is not much to do, and sometimes I look at it as I pass and that is as much as I can do, maybe it is enough, and maybe there will come a time when I will not need to have such a reminder of him so close by. Maybe the memory of him as I enter my last days will retreat into my heart more profoundly and I will not need help from any object in the room.

I knew, in their roughness, their way of moving in as though they were making a raid on space, that one of them would select this chair, would make it seem casual and thus all the more difficult to oppose. But I was waiting.

"Do not sit in that chair," I said when he had moved the table aside and pulled out the chair which I had carefully trapped against the wall so that it would not be defiled by my visitors. "You can use the one beside it but not that one."

"I cannot use a chair?" he enquired, as though addressing a fool. "What else are chairs for? I cannot sit on a chair?" The tone now was more insolent than menacing, but it had an element of menace.

"No one sits on that chair," I said quietly.

"No one?" he asked.

I made my voice even quieter.

"No one," I replied.

My two visitors looked at each other. I was waiting. I did not turn away from them and I tried to seem gentle, someone hardly worth defying, especially on what might have seemed to them like a whim, a woman's notion.

"Why not?" he asked, with a sort of sweet sarcasm.

"Why not?" he asked again as though I were a child.

I could hardly breathe now and I rested my hands on the back of the chair that was nearest me and I realized from the way my breath came and the sudden slowness in my heartbeat that it would not be long before all the life in me, the little left, would go, as a flame goes out on a mild day, easily, needing only the smallest hint of wind, a sudden flicker and then out, gone, as though it had never been alight.

"Don't sit there," I said quietly.

"But you must explain," he said.

"The chair," I said, "is left for someone who will not return."

"But he will return," he said.

"No," I replied, "he will not."

"Your son will return," he said.

"The chair is for my husband," I replied as if he this time

were the fool. I felt content when I said the name, as though the very saying of the word "husband" had pulled something back into the room, or a shadow of something, enough for me in any case, but not enough for them. And then he went to sit in the chair, he turned it towards himself, he was ready to perch there with his back to me.

I was waiting. Quickly, I found the sharp knife and I held it and touched the blade. I did not point it towards them, but my movement to reach for it had been so swift and sudden that I caught their attention. I glanced at them and then looked down at the blade.

"I have another one hidden," I said, "and if either of you touch the chair again, if you so much as touch it, I will wait, I am waiting now, and I will come in the night, I will move as silently as the air itself moves, and you will not have time to make a sound. Do not think for a moment that I will not do this."

I turned then as though I had work to do. I washed some jugs that did not need to be washed and then I asked them if they would get me water. I knew that they wanted to be alone with each other now and when they had gone out and I put the chair back against the wall and then the table against it. I knew that maybe it was time I forgot about the man I married as I would join him soon enough. Maybe it was time to consign this chair to nothing, but I would do this on a day when it was not important. I would break its spell in my own good time.

I move now between the things of this world that are precise, sharp and close by, and some bitter imaginings. On those Sabbath days once the prayers were intoned and God was thanked and praised, there was always time to wonder about what was beyond us in the sky or what world lay buried in the hollows of the earth. I had a sense on some of those days, after hours of silence, of my mother struggling to come towards me, reaching out from somewhere very dark, reaching towards me as though looking for food or drink. As darkness fell on those Sabbath days I saw her sinking back into a cavernous place, a huge, wide-mouthed space; over her were things flitting and flying and there was the sound of the rumbling earth beneath her. I do not know why I imagined this, and it would have been easier to imagine her slowly turning to dust in the warm earth close to the places that she loved. And it was always easy to switch from these musings on imagined places under the earth to the absorbing business of now, or the things that happened, or the figures who came in daylight to my door.

Marcus from Cana was not my cousin, although he called me his cousin because our mothers gave birth to us at the same time in adjoining houses. We played together and we grew up together until it was time for us to grow apart. When he came to the house in Nazareth I was alone. I had not seen him in years. I knew that he had gone to Jerusalem and I knew that he had greater talents than many others who had gone and that he had inherited from his father a mixture of shyness and stability, a way to impress people, fool them maybe if there was a need for that, and an ability to agree with everyone and have no opinions of his own on anything, or opinions of his own that he kept to himself.

Marcus appeared at my door and sat at my table. He did not want water or food and there was something new about him, something I would later notice when my protectors, or my guards, or whatever it is they are, came to this house—a coldness, a determination, an ability to use silence, a hardness around the eyes and the mouth which suggested a hardness in the heart. He told me what he had seen, and he told me what, even then, the consequences would be. He had not seen what he saw for no reason, he said; he had been asked by one of his colleagues to accompany him on the Sabbath day to the pool behind the sheep market in Jerusalem because it was known that this was where my son and his friends congregated. This was where, in Marcus's words, they caused a fuss and made a crowd gather and began to be noticed.

There was an old fool, Marcus said, who used to lie there among all the rest of them, the crippled, the withered, the blind, the lame and the halt, and they were mad enough to believe that at a certain season an angel came down into the pool and disturbed the water and whoever was the first in the pool after the troubling of the water would be cured of whatever disease he had. And my son and his friends, the young men he had come to the house with, were there that day. Marcus saw all the commotion he and his friends were making, whipping up hysteria among the crowds. They must have known, Marcus said, how carefully they were being watched. From all sides, he said, there were spies, informers, middle-men. They were open in their watching, perhaps their being paid or rewarded depended on their being seen to watch. Marcus said that he stood close to the pool, close enough to see that the focus of attention was this idiot, half beggar, half imbecile, who was roaring out that he had been crippled for many years. Marcus heard my son as everyone around came closer. "Wilt thou be made whole?" he was shouting. Some were laughing and doing imitations of his voice, but others were beckoning even more people to move silently towards the voice at the centre, near the pool, the voice booming "Wilt thou be made whole?" And the idiot began insisting that the angel was coming to trouble the water, but because he had no servant to help him, and only the first in the water could be cured, he was doomed to remain immobile for the rest of his days. And the voice rose up again, and this time no one laughed or mocked. There was complete silence from all around as this time the voice said "Take up thy bed and walk."

Marcus did not know for how long the silence lasted; he could see the man lying there and then the crowd pushed back and still no one spoke as the man stood up and my son told him that he was to sin no more. And then the man moved away, leaving the stretcher there. He made his way towards the Temple with a crowd following him, and my son and his friends following too. They were creating a frenzy on the Sabbath. In the Temple, no one cared about the man and why he was walking, but they cared that he was shouting and pointing and that there was a large crowd following him and that it was the Sabbath. No one, Marcus said, was in any doubt about who had caused this breach of the Sabbath. The only reason my son was not arrested then and there, Marcus said, was because he was being watched to see where he might go next and to see who was backing him. The authorities, both Jewish and Roman, wondered where he would take them, what would happen if they made sure that he went nowhere without spies and observers.

"Is there anything we can do," I asked, "to stop him?"

"Yes there is," Marcus said. "If he were to return home, return alone, and not even be seen on the street, not even work or have any visitors, just stay in these rooms, disappear, then that might save him, but even then he will be watched; but nothing else will work and if it happens, if he returns, then it must be soon."

And so I decided to set out for Cana for the wedding of my cousin's daughter, having decided previously that I would not go. I disliked weddings. I dislike the amount of laughter and talk and the waste of food and the drink flowing over and the bride and groom more like a couple to be sacrificed, for the sake of money, or status, or inheritance, to be singled out and celebrated for something that was none of anyone's business and then to be set up with roars of jollity and drunkenness and unnecessary gatherings of people. It was easier when you were young because somehow those days of smiling people and the general madness made your eyes dart in your head until you could come to love a buffoon if he came close enough.

I went to Cana not to celebrate the joining together with much clamour of two people, one of whom I barely knew and the other not at all, but to see if I could get my son home. For days before, I summoned what strength I had in my eyes and I practised with my voice, worked out ways of keeping it low and insistent. I prepared warnings and threats if promises would not do. There must be, I thought, one thing I could say that might matter. One sentence. One promise. One threat.

One warning. And I was sure as I sat there that I had it; I had fooled myself that he would come back with me, that he had had enough of wandering and that he was broken now, or that I could break him with some words.

When I arrived in Cana some days before the wedding I knew, or I almost knew, that I had come in vain. The only talk was the talk of him and the fact that I was his mother meant that I was noticed and approached.

Close to the house of my cousin Miriam was the house of Lazarus. I had known him since he was a baby. Of all the children that any of us had, he was, from the day he appeared in the world, the most beautiful. He seemed to smile before he did anything else. When we visited Ramira, his mother, she would put her fingers to her lips and take us across the room to where his cot lay and when we looked in he seemed to be already smiling. It made Ramira at times almost embarrassed because when we came to visit we would discover that we were not alone in feeling that we had come to visit the boy as he learned to walk and talk as much we had come to see his parents or his sisters. Instantly, as soon as other children saw him, they wanted him in their game; whatever they did once he was there became peaceful and harmonious. I now know that he was alone among us in possessing something strange—he had not been visited by darkness or by fear, by what comes into our spirits in the deepest part of the night or the end of the Sabbath and lurks there. There were years when I did not see him, the years when the family moved to Bethany before they returned to live in Cana, but I always heard the news and it always included something about him—how he was growing up golden and graceful, serious and kind, and how worried they were because they knew they would not be able to keep him among the olive groves and the fruit trees, that something would happen to him, that a great city would call to him, that the charm he exuded and his beauty, grown manly now, would need another realm in which to flourish.

But no one realized that it would be the realm of death he was destined for, that all the grace and beauty, all of his aura of specialness, like a gift from the gods to his parents and his sisters, that all of it was a grim joke, like being teased by a smell of delicious food or the possibility of plenty, when it was really only something passing by, destined for elsewhere. I know that he moaned in pain for a day or two and then he was better and then the pains came again, and they came in his head and they often lasted through the night and that he cried out, he cried out that he would promise to be good. But there was nothing to be done, there was poison growing in his head, he began to weaken and he could not bear light, even a chink of light. If the door opened as someone came into the room, it would be enough for him, he would cry out. I do not know for how long this went on; I know that they cared for him and I know too that it was as though a golden harvest had been mowed down by a night's dark wind, or a pestilence had come into the trees and shrunk the fruit, and it was unlucky even to mention his name or ask for news of him.

So I did not ask for news of him but I often thought of him, especially as I prepared to come to Cana. I wondered if I should visit him or his sisters. As I set out, I did not know that he had already died.

When I arrived in Cana there was a strange emptiness in the streets. I heard afterwards that for two hours or more some days earlier the birds had withdrawn from the air as though it were night or there were some cataclysm in progress that meant danger to them and made them retreat into their nests. And there was a hushed holding-in of things, no wind, no rustling in the leaves of trees, no animal sounds. Cats moved out of sight, and shadows—even the very shadows—stayed as they were. Lazarus had died a week earlier, and then when he was four days in his grave my son and his followers had reached Cana with their high-flown talk. And when my son told them to dig Lazarus up, remove him from his tomb, no one wanted to do this. In the days before he died Lazarus had become peaceful and beautiful. No one wanted to touch him now, disturb him in the ground, but so great was the frenzy at the arriving horde that his sisters had no choice. The crowd had arrived with news of a blind man who could see and of a gathering where there was no food and which had, as though by a miracle, been filled with plenty. The talk was of nothing except power and miracles. It was as if the crowd was roaming the countryside like a swarm of locusts in search of want and affliction.

But no one among them thought that anyone could raise the dead. It had occurred to no one. Most of them believed, or so I learned, that it should not even be tried, that it would represent a mockery of the sky itself. They felt, as I felt, as I still feel, that no one should tamper with the fullness that is death. Death needs time and silence. The dead must be left alone with their new gift or their new freedom from affliction.

I know, because Marcus told me, that Mary and Martha, the two sisters of the dead boy, began to follow my son once they had heard the news of the lame walking and the blind seeing. And I understand that they would have done anything in those last silent days. They watched helplessly as their brother grew easily towards death in the same way as a source for a river, hidden under the earth, begins flowing and carries water across a plain to the sea. They would have done anything to divert the stream, make it meander on the plain and dry up under the weight of the sun. They would have done anything to keep their brother alive. They sent word to my son and they asked him to come but he did not. It was something I learned when I saw him myself, that, if the time was not right, he would not be disturbed by a merely human voice, or the pleadings of anyone he knew. Thus he paid no attention to what he heard from Martha and Mary and they stayed with their brother so they would be with him when he took his last breath, when he was fully part of the waves of the sea, an invisible aspect of their rhythm. And during those days then, as river water slowly took on the taste of salt and they buried him and he lay fresh in the earth, many people who had loved Lazarus and who had known his sisters came to the house to comfort them. There was talk and lamentation.

And then when they heard that the crowd had arrived, like a carnival with every malcontent and half-crazed soothsayer following in its wake, Martha went out into the streets to announce her brother's death to my son. She confronted him and won silence from him and those around him and she cried out "If you had been here he would not have died." And she was ready to go further, but stopped for a moment when she saw how sorry he was, when she saw how he knew, or seemed to know, that the suffering and death of Lazarus was a sadness almost too great for anyone to bear. And now it was a weight that could not be lifted.

Having let the silence linger for some moments, Martha spoke again as the crowd listened. She spoke very quietly, but what she said was heard. She was so desperate in her grief that her pleading sounded like a challenge.

"I know," she said, "that even now that he is four days in the earth, you have the power to raise him."

"He will rise," my son replied, "as all mankind will rise, when time relents, when the sea itself becomes a glassy stillness."

"No," Martha said, "you have the power to do it now."

And she told my son then what the others had told him, that he was not a mortal as we are mortal, but she believed that he was God's son, that he had been sent to us in mortal guise, but he was not mortal and he had powers, that he was the one we had been waiting for, who would be king on earth and in the skies, and that she and her sister had been among those blessed enough to recognize him, as they recognized him now. For the sake of her brother, she told him in plain loud words, with her arms spread out wide, that he was the son of God.

When Martha found Mary, who had returned to the grave to weep there, she too went to my son and told him that he had the power. As she wept, so did he, because he had known Lazarus all of his life and had loved him as all of us did, and he came with her to the grave, freshly covered with earth, and there was a murmuring from the crowd that had followed, people shouting that if he could heal the sick and make the crippled walk and the blind see, then he could raise the dead.

He stood there silently for a time and then in a voice like a whisper he ordered the grave to be dug up while Martha, screaming now, afraid that what she had asked for was being granted, cried that they had suffered enough and the body would be stinking and rotting after its time in the earth, but my son insisted and the crowd stood by as the grave was opened and the soft earth lifted from where it lay over Lazarus's body. Once the body could be seen, most of the onlookers had moved away in horror and fright, all except Martha and Mary and my son, who called out the words: "Lazarus come forth." And gradually the crowd came close again to the grave, and this was the time when the birdsong ceased and the birds withdrew from the air. Martha believed too that time was then suspended, that in those two hours nothing grew, nothing was born or came into being, nothing died or withered in any way.

Slowly, the figure dirtied with clay and covered in grave-clothes wound around him began with great uncertainty to move in the place they had made for him. It was as though the earth beneath him was pushing him and then letting him be still in his great forgetfulness and nudging him again like some strange new creature jerking and wriggling towards life. He was bound with the sheets and his face was covered with a napkin and now he turned as a child in the freshness of the womb who turns knowing that his time there is up and he must wrestle his way into the world. "Loose him and let him go," my son said, and two men came, two neighbours, and they stood in the grave as those around watched in hushed amazement and fright as they lifted Lazarus and then unbound him. He stood up with merely a cloth around his waist.

He had been unchanged by death. Once his eyes opened, he stared at the sun with a deep unearthly puzzlement and then at the sky around the sun. He seemed not to see the crowd; some sounds came from him, not words exactly, something closer to whispered cries, or whimpers, and then the crowd stood back as Lazarus moved through them, past them, looking at no one, being led by his sisters back to their house, the world around remaining stilled and silent, and my son too, I am told, stilled and silent, as Lazarus began to weep.

At first they noticed just the tears, but then his crying came in howls as his two sisters led him gently towards the house, followed all the way by the silent crowd as the howling grew louder and more fierce. By the time they reached their door he could barely walk. They disappeared inside and closed the shutters from the burning sun and did not appear again that day, despite the waiting crowd who lingered hour after hour, even as night fell, and some indeed through the night itself and even as the morning came.

There was in those first days a strange atmosphere in Cana. I noticed the stalls and the stallholders had more things on display than ever before, not merely food and clothes, but also cooking utensils and locks for doors. And there were animals for sale—monkeys, birds, like jungle birds, gorgeous creatures coloured red and yellow and blue, of a brightness I had never seen before, causing a crowd to gather around them in wonder. And there was a levity about the stallholders and those who walked the streets, as though some burden had been lifted, and there was much calling and yelling and figures on street corners guffawing. Even in Jerusalem on market days, when I used to go to that place before I was married, there had always been a gravity, a sense of people doing business who meant business, or preparing themselves with due decorum for the Sabbath. But Cana was full of raised voices and raised dust, sly laughter, young men laughing without restraint, the air full of whistling and cat-calls. As soon as my cousin Miriam and I removed ourselves indoors, she told me the story of what had happened to Lazarus, and how no one now would even pass the house near by, where he and his sisters lived, but would cross the street instead, and how she believed that he was in bed in a darkened room, that she had heard that he could barely swallow water and barely hold down soft bread which had been soaked in water. The hordes had moved on, she said, followed by an even larger caravan of hucksters, salesmen, water-carriers, fire-eaters and purveyors of cheap food. All were being watched with a ferocious zeal by the authorities, some of whom were in disguise, but others of whom were following openly and then quickly departing for Jerusalem to be the first to arrive with word of some new outrage, some new miracle, some new breach in the great order that was maintained to keep the Romans pleased.

Miriam had sent word to my son that I was in Cana and word had come back that he would be at the wedding and his place would be beside his mother. Then, I thought, we could speak. I remained calm. I dozed and then slept deeply after my journey. I listened to Miriam go over and over the story of Lazarus. I was ready to confront my son and ready also to keep him in one of the inner rooms of Miriam's house until things grew calm, until some other novelty arrived on the scene, and we could slip quietly back to Nazareth. I noticed in the night before the wedding that the streets around Miriam's house, normally so quiet once darkness fell, were filled with the sounds of feet and voices. All through the night I heard them, men moving fearlessly, laughing and talking, or calling to each other, or having mock fights or funny arguments and then running back and forth on the street.

Also, that night, before we went to bed, people came to the house, almost hysterical with news of the bride, the lavish gifts she had received, the clothes she would wear. There was much discussion of the bridegroom's family and divisions within it over protocol and tradition. I did not speak, but I knew that I was noticed and felt that some people had come to the house to peer at me, or be in my presence. As soon as I could I left the room to help in the kitchen. When I returned with a tray to collect empty cups, I stood for a second in the doorway, in the shadows where no one noticed me, and I heard Miriam and one other woman recount once more to others the story of Lazarus.

It struck me on hearing something each of them said that neither of them had actually been there. Later, when I found Miriam alone, I asked her if she had personally been in the crowd that day and she smiled and said no, but she had heard all the details from several who had witnessed it all. On seeing my expression then, she turned to the window and closed the shutters and spoke quietly.

"I know Lazarus died. Do not doubt that he died. And that he had been buried for four days. Do not doubt that. And he is alive now, he will be at the wedding tomorrow. And there is a new strangeness; no one, not one of us, knows what the next event will be. There is talk of a revolt against the Romans, or a revolt against the teachers. Some people say that the Romans wish to overthrow the teachers, and others that the teachers are behind it all, but it is also possible that there will be no revolt or indeed that there will be one against everything we have known before, including death itself."

She repeated the words "including death itself." The force of her words held me still.

"Including death itself," she said again. "Lazarus may be merely the first. But he is alive now in his own house and I can swear to you that one week ago he was dead. This may be what we have waited for, and that is why the crowd has come here and there are men shouting in the night."

In the kitchen the next morning news came that Martha, Mary and Lazarus were going to come to Miriam's house first, and then accompany us to the feast. Lazarus was still weak, we were told, and his sisters had become aware of how afraid people were of him. "He lives with the secret that none of us knows," Miriam said. "His spirit had time to take root in the other world, and people are afraid of what he could say, the knowledge he could impart. His sisters do not want to go alone with him to the wedding."

I dressed carefully. The day was hot and the interior of the house was kept dark. We moved slowly in the dense and humid air. Miriam and I found ourselves several times in the main room of the house alone together, uneasy with each other, but not stirring from our chairs and not speaking. We were both waiting for the visitors to come. A few times when we heard sounds we both looked at each other ominously, fearfully. Neither of us knew what would happen when Martha and Mary led their brother into this room. And, as time went by, our wondering became more tense. Finally, in the stillness and the heat and the silence, I fell asleep and when I woke Miriam was standing over me, whispering "They are here. They have finally arrived."

The sisters looked more beautiful than I had ever seen them. In their solemnity as they entered the closeness of the room and approached me, they were figures of substance, grandeur, immense dignity. It was as though they had been marked and separated from others by what they had been through, it came across in their poise, a depth in the expression on their faces when they smiled. As they both came towards me I realized that I was associated in their minds with what had occurred and that they wished to touch me, embrace me, thank me, as if I had something to do with the fact that their brother was alive.

Their brother stood in the doorway and then moved quietly into the room. When he sighed all of us moved towards him and it was then, just then, that the opportunity came and it was the only one I had, and I think it may have been the only opportunity anyone had, to ask him. It was the semi-darkness of the room, the stillness of the air and the fact that all of us, us four women, would know to keep silent about what we should not speak of. There were a few seconds in which any one of us could have asked him about the cave full of souls where he had been. Was it a place of massive, obliterating darkness, or was there light? Of wakefulness, or of dreams, or of deep sleep? Were there voices, or was there pure stillness, or some other sound like the dripping of water, or sighs, or echoes? Did he know anyone? Did he meet his mother, whom we all had loved?

Did he remember us as he wandered in the place where he had been? Was there blood or pain? Was it a landscape of dull, washed colours, or a red vastness, with cliffs, or forests, or deserts, or encroaching mist? Was anyone afraid? Did he wish to return there?

Lazarus stood in the darkened room and sighed again and something was broken, the great chance had escaped us, maybe never to return. Miriam asked him if he wanted water and he nodded. His sisters led him to a chair and he sat alone, utterly isolated. He seemed to be reaching deep into himself for some soft energy which had been left to him and which kept him awake, his sisters said, both day and night.

He did not speak as we set out for the wedding. It was hard not to watch him as he was being helped along by his sisters, moving as though his spirit was still filled with the thunderous novelty of its own great death, like a pitcher of sweet water filled to the brim, heavy with itself. I was so involved in watching him and then trying to look away that I had put no thought into what was ahead until we came close to the house where the wedding feast was to take place and I saw a crowd who I knew had nothing to do with the wedding, not only hawkers and hucksters I had seen before, but young men in large groups, all of them arguing and shouting. Everybody stood back as we approached; a slow silence came over the crowd. I thought at first it was solely because Lazarus was among us, still being led by both of his sisters. But then I realized that the silence was also for me and I wished I had not come here. I did not know how these people knew who I was. That they should stand back for me struck me as almost funny, something I might dream, but it was not funny, it was frightening when I saw the mixture of respect and fear in their eyes so I looked down at the dust and made my way into the wedding feast with my friends as though I was nobody.

Immediately, I was separated from the others and taken to a table which ran along a covered shaded space where I was placed beside Marcus who seemed to have been waiting there for me. He told me that he could not stay, that it would be dangerous now for anyone to be seen with us, and he pointed to a figure standing casually at the entrance, whom we must have passed on the way in, although I had not noticed him.

"Watch him," Marcus said. "He is one of the two or three figures who move easily between the Jewish leaders and the Romans, that is what he is paid to do. He owns olive groves that run through a whole stretch of valley and he has many assistants and servants and a house of great luxury. He seldom has any reason to leave Jerusalem except when he visits his own land. He is a man without scruples. He comes from the most humble place and the most humble circumstances. He rose at first not because of his wit but because he can strangle a man without leaving a mark or making a sound. That is what he was used for, but now he has other uses. He will decide what must happen and he will be listened to. His judgment will be dispassionate, merciless. The fact that he is here at all means that all of you are lost unless you move with very great care. You must return home as soon as possible. Both you and your son. You and the one they are watching most must slip away from here even before the feast starts and if you can disguise him in some way all the better, but you must not speak to anyone or stop and he must not leave the house for months, maybe even years. It is the only chance that you have."

refresh myself and that will be the signal. You must follow me. You must tell no one that you are going. You must leave alone."

Even before I had finished speaking, he had moved away from me.

"Woman, what have I to do with thee?" he asked, and then again louder so that it was heard all around. "Woman, what have I to do with thee?"

"I am your mother," I said. But by this time he had begun to talk to others, high flown talk and riddles, using strange proud terms to describe himself and his task in the world. I heard him saying—I heard it then and I noticed how heads bowed all around when he said it—I heard him saying that he was the Son of God.

As he sat down I wondered if he was pondering what I had whispered to him, if once the bride and bridegroom appeared I should make a move and then wait for him, but slowly, as we waited, and more and more people came to touch him, and as news spread of the numbers who were outside, I realized that he had not even heard me. He heard no one in the excitement of that time. And when the bride and bridegroom came and the cheering began, I had to work out what I should do. I decided that I would stay with him now and I would seek out another chance, maybe when night fell or in the early morning there might be a time that he would be alone and open to warnings. And then it struck me as I looked at him again how ignorant and foolish and meek and ill-informed I would seem warning him as if I knew more than he did. I wished just then that Marcus had not gone, but as I glanced over towards the entrance I could see why he had—the man, the strangler, was standing there but now he had two or three men with him, men stronger-looking than he was and he was pointing to figures in the crowd. In that second he caught my eye again and I became even more frightened than when I heard the words about the Son of God: I understood that I had not missed my chance to take my son away from here, I understood that I never had such a chance in the first place and that all of us were doomed.

I did not eat much and I do not remember the food. Although my son and I sat beside each other for more than two hours, we did not speak. It seems odd now, but there was nothing strange about our silence. So great was the heightened atmosphere and the sense of growing hysteria, with shouting coming from outside, that mere speech between two people would have been like crumbs on the floor. In the same way as Lazarus had a glow of death about him, almost like a garb that covered every aspect of his being and that no one could penetrate, so too with my son there was a sense of the fluster of life, the bright sky on a windy day, or the trees when they were filled with ripe, unharvested fruit, a sense of an unthinking energy, like bounty. He was so far from the child I remembered or the young boy who seemed happiest in the morning when I came to him and spoke to him as the day began. He was beautiful then and delicate and awash with needs. There was nothing delicate about him now, he was all displayed manliness, utterly confident and radiant, yes, radiant like light is radiant, so that there was nothing we could have spoken of then in those hours, it would have been like speaking to the stars or the full moon.

At some point I noticed that more people had gained entrance to the feast and that all of the attention seemed to be focused on our table rather than on the table where the bride and bridegroom sat. I noticed Martha and Mary leading Lazarus out, linking him, almost holding him, and I noticed the strangler still there, but I was careful now not to catch his eye. And then someone began to shout that the wine had run out and a number of them approached our table; they were the new people who had come and they had about them a sort of ragged excitement, a look on their faces that was trusting and imploring, and a ring in their voices now that was mildly hysterical. More of them began to shout that there was no wine left, some of them even focusing their attention on me, as though I could do something about it. I outstared them and when they shouted louder I pretended that I did not hear them. I may have sipped some wine but it was a matter of indifference to me whether there was any left or not. I wondered indeed if some of the men standing in front of our table had not had enough wine. But my son stood up and spoke to those around him, asking that six stone containers full of water be brought to him. What was strange then was how quickly those containers were carried into the room. I do not know whether each one contained water or wine, certainly the first one contained water, but in all the shouting and confusion no one knew what happened until they began to shout that he had changed the water into wine. They begged for the bridegroom and the bride's father to come and sample the new wine as one of them began to proclaim how strange and unusual it was for the host to have kept the good wine until last. And then a vast cheering went up and everyone at the feast began to applaud.

No one noticed, however, that I did not cheer. But in the noise around us I was being included somehow as if my presence had helped to change water into wine. Once it had died down and most people had gone back to their places, I decided

that I would speak one more time. I said again what I had said
before but I tried to put a great urgency into my words. "You
are in great danger," I began but I saw immediately that it was
no use, and without thinking I stood up and, as though my
departure were casual and I would soon return, I left the feast
and went back to Miriam's house. I took my belongings and
made my way back to Nazareth.

And I thought then that that was the worst part, because
when I walked to where I would find the convoy coming back
home, I found it empty. There was no one to ask, and there was
no shelter. It was the only place I knew and I waited although
the sun was hot. After a while I found shade under a small
thin tree and waited longer, but the shade was no use when
the rain came. The sky had been so blue, the day so hot; the
change now was sudden and total. The rain beat down, and
the wind blew. There was nowhere you could go to avoid it.
I did what I could. I covered up and huddled under the tree.
I waited and others slowly began to gather too, even though
the rain persisted and there was thunder. They said that there
would be a convoy, and that there was no other place to wait.
I stayed there, soaked by rain, because I had no choice. I knew
that I had some dry clothes in my bag and hoped that I could
change into them when the rain stopped. I would have to wait
through the night. There was a man selling food so I did not go
hungry. Gradually, it became calm and I changed my clothes
and I must have slept for a while and woke then to sounds, to
the sounds of animals, and other travellers' voices, and we set
out then in the hour before dawn. I did not know what I would
do when I reached home, but it seemed to me then as we set
out that I did not have a choice. But it was always there, it

was there from the moment I stood up from the table—that I could turn back.

Sometimes, as we were moving, I imagined turning, asking them to stop, and waiting, waiting for the next convoy which would come and lead me back from where I had fled. For what? To do what? Maybe to be there so I could see what others were seeing. Maybe to stay close if they would let me stay close. To ask nothing. To watch. To know. I did not put words on it then. But I let it come to me even as we set out. We had been travelling for some time when I knew that I would have to make a decision. At one of the stops I saw a convoy coming in the distance which could have led me back and as I watched them approach I decided that I would not speak to them. I would complete the journey I had begun towards home.

I thought that it would be quiet when I returned, and that I would remain undisturbed. As much as I could, I put out of my mind what I had seen and heard. I spent my days easily, I prayed in the morning as I had always done, I went out once a day to draw water and feed the animals and tend the garden and the trees, and went further every few days to make sure that I had whatever kindling and firewood were necessary. But I did not need much. When it was bright I sat alone in the shadowy spaces of the house. I did not respond to any callers. I did not respond even when three of the Elders from the Synagogue came and called my name several times, banging loudly on the door. And when it was dark I lay down on the bed and sometimes I slept. Gradually, despite my solitude, I came to realize that the house was marked and I was noticed and watched as I tended the goats or fed the chickens. When I went to get water, people at the well stepped aside as I approached, allowed me through with my water-carrier and remained silent until I had turned towards home away. When I slipped into the Synagogue, women moved aside for me but were careful not to sit close to me. But a few women spoke to me, some news came to me. It was a strange period during which I tried not to think, or imagine, or dream, or even remember, when the thoughts that came arrived unbidden and were to do with time—time that turns a baby who is so defenceless into a small boy, with a boy's fears, insecurities and petty cruelties, and then creates a young man, someone with his own words and thoughts and secret feelings.

And then time created the man who sat beside me at the wedding feast of Cana, the man not heeding me, hearing no one, a man filled with power, a power that seemed to have no memory of years before, when he needed my breast for milk, my hand to help steady him as he learned to walk, or my voice to soothe him to sleep.

And what was strange about the power he exuded was that it made me love him and seek to protect him even more than I did when he had no power. It was not that I saw through it or did not believe it. It was not that I saw him still as a child. No, I saw a power fixed and truly itself, formed. I saw something that seemed to have no history and to have come from nowhere, and I sought in my dreams and in my waking time to protect it and I felt an abiding love for it. For him, whatever he had become. I believe that I listened to very few people but I must have listened to someone in the street or at the well because I learned that his followers had gone out on a ship. They sailed out on a ship at the time when my son had disappeared into the mountains, at a time when he had refused whatever demands he made on them to lead them further, when he fled not with me as I had implored him to do, but alone because he too must have seen the signs and the dangers. His followers, I was told, had taken an old boat on the sea and set out for some reason of their own towards Capernaum. It was dark and the sea began to rise by reason of a great sudden wind; it blew the vessel, which was too full, backwards and forwards and filled it with water as it was pulled each way, so that all of his followers felt they would drown. It was then, I was told, that he appeared to them in the moonlight and he was, or so my neighbours murmured that he was, actually walking on the water as though it were smooth dry land. And by his power he was calming the waves. He was doing what no one else could do. There must have been other stories, and perhaps this one I heard only in part, perhaps something else happened, or perhaps there was no wind, or he calmed the wind. I do not know. I put no thought into it.

I know that one day as I stood at the well a woman came and said that he could end the world if he wanted or make things grow to twice their size and I know that I turned away from her without filling my water jug and I walked back to the house and did not come out until the following day. I lived in a haze of waiting, trying still not to think or remember. I moved quietly within the four walls of the house or the garden or the fields. I needed very little nourishment. Sometimes one of the neighbours left food hanging from a hook by the side wall and when night fell I collected it. One day, when the knocking was louder and more insistent than usual and there was a man's voice shouting, I heard the neighbours gathering in the road and telling whoever it was that there was no one inside. When the voice asked if this was not the house of my son and if I did not live within these walls, the neighbours told him yes, but that the house was empty now and locked and no one had been near it for some time. I stood on the inside of the door, listening, barely breathing, hardly making a sound.

I waited and weeks went by. Sometimes I did hear news. I knew that he had not gone to the mountains again and I knew also that Lazarus was still alive and, indeed, had become a subject for intense discussion at every well and every street corner, at every place where people gathered. I knew that people now waited outside Lazarus's house to catch a glimpse of him, that all of the fear of him had gone. For those who gathered and gossiped it was a high time, filled with rumours and fresh news, filled with stories both true and wildly exaggerated. I lived mostly in silence, but somehow the wildness that was in the very air, the air in which the dead had been brought back to life and water changed into wine and the very waves of the sea made calm by a man walking on water, this great disturbance in the world made its way like creeping mist or dampness in the two or three rooms I inhabited.

When Marcus came I was expecting him. I heard knocking for a while and then I heard him asking a neighbour where I was. I opened the door for him. The shadows were gathering, but I did not light a lamp; it was a month or more since I had used a lamp. I offered him a chair at the table and then some water and some fruit. I told him to tell me what he could. He said that there was only one thing he had to tell me and I should be ready to hear the worst. He said that a decision had been made to deal with the situation. He stopped for a moment and I thought it might be that my son would be banished or commanded not to appear in public or speak again. But I stood up and went towards the door and, for what reason I do not know, made as though to leave the house so I would not have to hear what he would now say. But I did not reach the door in time. He spoke flatly, firmly.

"He is to be crucified," he said.

I turned and I knew from his statement that there was only one question to be asked.

"When?"

"Within a short time," he said. "He has moved back towards the centre of power and there are even more followers. The authorities know where he is and they can capture him at any time."

And then I found myself asking a foolish question, but a question I had to ask.

"Is there anything that can be done to stop this?"

"No," he said, "but you must leave here as soon as it is dawn. They will come looking for all his followers."

"I am not one of his followers," I said.

"You must believe me when I say that they will come looking for you. You must leave."

I remained standing and I asked him what he would do.

"I will leave now but I can give you an address where you will be safe in Jerusalem."

"Where I will be safe?" I asked.

"You will be safe for the moment in Jerusalem."

"Where is my son?"

"Close to Jerusalem. The site for the crucifixion has been chosen. It will be near the city. If there is any chance for him, it will be there, but I have been told that there is no chance and that there has been no chance for some time. They have been waiting."

I had seen a crucifixion once, carried out by the Romans on one of their own. It was in the distance and I remember thinking that it was the most foul and frightening image that had ever been conjured up by men. I remember thinking also that I was old and getting older and that I hoped I would die before I ever saw anything like that again. It stayed with me, the sight in the distance, and it made me shiver and I had tried to think of another subject to obliterate the memory of this, the unspeakable image, the vast, fierce cruelty of it. But I did not know precisely how the victim died or how long it took, if they used spears or tortured them while they were hanging there or if something else, such as the hot sun, caused the body to expire over time. Of all the things I had thought about in my life it was the one that was furthest from me. It had nothing to do with me and I believed that I would never witness it again or come close to it in any way. I found myself now asking Marcus how long a crucifixion takes as though it were something surprising but ordinary too. He replied "Days maybe, but sometimes hours, it depends."

"On what?" I asked.

"Don't ask," he said. "It's better if you don't ask."

He left me then, apologizing that he could not travel with me, that if anything could be done he would need to keep his involvement with me distant and private. He advised me to wear a cloak and move carefully and be sure, as I travelled, that

I was not being followed. Before he left, I asked him to wait for one more minute. There was something about his briskness, his businesslike way of dealing with this, that had unsettled me.

"How do you know all this?" I asked him.

"I have informers," he said solemnly, almost proudly. "People who are well placed."

"And it has been decided?" I asked.

He nodded. I had a sensation that if I could think of one more question to ask, one more thing to say, the meaning would shift and soften. He waited at the door to see what I wanted to say now.

"Will I find him if I go to Jerusalem?" I asked.

"At the address I have given you," he replied, "they will know more than I do."

I almost asked him then why I should trust someone who knew more than he did, but I watched him as he hesitated at the door, and even in the last second before he finally departed I thought there was one more thing I should have asked or said. One more thing. But I could not think what it was. And then he went, and perhaps because there had been no one in this house for so long, he left behind a smell of pure unease. And the more I sat alone the more I realized that, for whatever reason, I should not go to the address he had given me, that I would return to Cana, to Miriam, and then I would find Martha and Mary, and I would ask them what to do.

I dressed as he told me to dress, wearing a cloak. I kept my voice low if I had to speak. I found a convoy moving towards

Cana and I joined it and I rested when the others rested and I was careful not to remain apart in case they noticed me too much. The talk was freer than I had heard before, and it was against the Romans, the Pharisees, the Elders, against the Temple itself, against laws and taxes. And women spoke almost as much as men. It was like living in a new time. And then the talk turned to the miracles my son and his followers could do, and how many were desperate to follow them now, or merely to find where they were.

Already, what was to occur weighed on me. At times, however, I forgot about it, I let my mind linger over anything at all only to find that what I was moving towards was waiting to spring as a frightened animal will spring. It came like that, in sudden jolts and shocks. And then it came more slowly, more insidiously. It entered my consciousness, it edged its way into me as something poisonous will crawl along the ground. On one of the nights during my journey I wandered out under the sky which was lit with stars and I believed for a moment that soon these stars would cease to glitter, that the nights of the future would be dark beyond dark, that the world itself would undergo a great change, and then I quickly came to see that the change would happen only to me and to the few who knew me; it would be only us who would look at the sky at night in the future and see the darkness before we saw the glitter. We would see the glittering stars as false and mocking, or as bewildered themselves by the night as we were, as left-over things confined to their place, their shining nothing more than a sort of pleading. I must have slept on those nights, and soon there was no time when what I was moving towards did not fix itself in my waking and my dreams, did not take over every thought.

* * *

Miriam had already heard rumours and I could see by the fear in her eyes when I arrived that she did not want to tell me what they were. I told her that I knew. And that was why I had come. But she still seemed uneasy. She did not move beyond the hallway of the house and left the door ajar while I stood there and it struck me then that she was not going to allow me beyond where she stood, that she was in fact blocking my entrance.

"What do you know?" I asked.

"I know," she said, "that they are rounding up all his friends and followers."

"Are you afraid?"

"Would you not be?"

"Do you want me to leave?"

She did not flinch.

"Yes, I do."

"Now?"

She nodded and whatever it was about the expression on her face and her posture and the aura she gave off I knew in that split second more than I had known before. I knew that I was facing into something ferocious and exact, something dark and evil beyond anyone's comprehension. I expected to be taken there and then at the door, dragged away somewhere, never to be seen in the world again. I understood everything then, and I almost cried aloud except that I was sure that Miriam would have done something to stop me. Instead, I thanked her and turned. I knew that I would not see her again in my life and I made my way to the house of Martha and Mary and I was ready to be turned away by them too.

They were waiting for me. Their brother lay again in a darkened room and could not speak. His sleep was peppered with moans and cries. Martha said his howls and cries in the hour before dawn harrowed up the soul of anyone who heard them. I told Martha and Mary of Marcus's visit and what had happened in the house of my cousin Miriam. I explained that I may even have been watched and followed, and that I was ready to walk out of their house without delay. They told me that they also believed that their house was watched and that one of them would have to stay, but they had already decided that if I came to them looking for help, then Mary would accompany me to Jerusalem, we would both slip away under cover of night. Even if we were followed there was nothing we could do except work out a way to evade our followers. And then I saw the difference between the two sisters as Martha told me that she knew he was to be judged by Pilate and that he was to be offered to the multitude to see if they wanted his release, but instructions had been issued by the Elders, she said, so it would mean nothing. Both the Romans and the Elders wanted him dead, but both were afraid to declare this openly.

Mary argued that something new would happen which would make such judgments and predictions meaningless, that the world's time had come and these days would be the last days and the days of the beginning. As she spoke, I dreamed of us escaping somewhere, to anywhere. I dreamed of taking my son through the crowd, him meek, humbled and oddly afraid, moving carefully, his eyes cast down, his followers all dispersed. But the Temple had the people in the square, Martha insisted again, they had ordered them to call for the release instead of the thief Barabbas, and the people would do what they had been told to do. My son would not be freed.

"He is already in custody," Martha said, "and it is already determined what is to be done with him."

They both watched me now, afraid to say the word which had not been uttered yet.

"You mean he will be crucified?" I asked.

"Yes," Martha said. "Yes."

And then Mary spoke: "But that will be the beginning."

"Of what?" I asked.

"Of a new life for the world," she said.

Martha and I ignored her.

"Is there anything that can be done?" I asked Martha.

Both of them appeared perplexed now and Martha nodded in the direction of the room where Lazarus lay.

"Ask my brother. My sister is right. We are coming to the end of the world," she said. "Or the world as we know it is coming to an end. Anything can happen. You must go to Jerusalem."

We found lodgings in the city. It seemed strange to me as I passed each person, or saw groups of people to whom I would never speak, whom I would never know and thought how odd it was that we looked the same, or appeared the same, moved on the same earth and spoke the same language and yet we shared nothing now, not one of them knew what I felt, or shared anything with me. They looked utterly apart and alien. It seemed astonishing to me that I carried a burden that no one could instantly see, that I must have looked ordinary to everybody I saw who did not know me, that everything was held inside.

I realized that we were lodging in a house filled with his followers, the ones who had not been arrested, that Mary had been told to take me here and she assured me that I would be protected, that the house was safe even if it did not seem so. I wonder how did she know this and she smiled and said that witnesses would be needed.

"By whom?" I asked. "For what?"

"Do not ask," she said. "You must trust me."

On our first night the door was locked by one of those who had come to our house in Nazareth years before; he eyed me coldly and suspiciously.

My son was already in custody, a real prisoner. He had allowed himself to be taken, and in this house during the hours that I spent with his followers they all seemed to feel that this was planned, part of a great deliverance that would take place in the world. I wanted to ask them if this deliverance would mean that he would not then be crucified, that he would be released, but they all, including Mary, once she was in their company, spoke in a maze of riddles. No question asked, I knew, would elicit a straight answer. I was back in the world of fools, twitchers, malcontents, stammerers, all of them hysterical now and almost out of breath with excitement even before they spoke. And within this group of men I noticed that there was a set of hierarchies, men who spoke and were listened to, for example, or whose presence created silence, or who sat at the top of the table, or who felt free to ignore me and my companion and who demanded food from the other women who scampered in and out of the room like hunched and obedient animals.

*   *   *

The next day, all of us left the house. One of the men, the one who comes here still, was given control of Mary and myself. He told us to stay with him at all times and speak to no one. We moved through the narrow streets in the morning until we came to a vast open space filled with people.

"All of these people," our minder told me, "are in the pay of the Temple. All of them are here to shout for the freedom of the thief when the moment comes. Pilate knows this, the Temple knows that it will succeed, and it is possible that even the thief has been told. It is the beginning of our redemption, the great new dawn for the world. It is mapped out as the sea and the land are mapped out."

By the time he finished speaking I was tired of walking, one of my shoes hurt. As I closed my eyes and listened, I noticed that there was something about his voice and his tone; I felt that he did not mean what he said, but had learned it and come to believe it was all the more true and impressive because of that.

It was hard to credit that everything in the square had been arranged, but there was a different atmosphere here than there had been in the streets of Cana or at the wedding itself—there were no sudden shouts or shifts of mood, no sense of a wild-eyed gathering of people. Many of those in the square were older; they came in smaller groups. None of them seemed to recognize us, but nonetheless we stood in the shadows, Mary and I trying to appear as though this was a normal place for us to come, or as though we too with our minder were part of the arrangement.

At first I could not hear what was being said from the balcony of the building across the square and it was difficult even to get a clear view. We had to move from the shadows into the sun and then push forward into the crowd. It was Pilate, everyone around murmured his name, and he was shouting louder each time he spoke.

"What accusation bring ye against this man?"

And the people were shouting back in one voice.

"If he were not a malefactor, we would not have delivered him up to thee!"

I missed the next moment as someone had pushed me to the side and there was too much talking around us but Mary heard it and she told me what it was. Pilate had asked the crowd to take the prisoner and deal with him according to Jewish law.

Pilate was still alone on the balcony with one or two officials standing to the side. Now I heard the response of the crowd because it came in ringing tones.

"It is not lawful to put any man to death," they said, and it was clear in how they said it that all of this, every moment we were witnessing, had indeed been arranged. I did not know that such things could happen. Then Pilate disappeared and a new feeling grew among those around us, the talking and muttering ceased and I felt something fresh coming into the atmosphere as all of us stared in the direction of the balcony. I sensed a thirst for blood among the crowd. I could see it in people's faces, how their jaws were set and their eyes were bright with excitement. There was a dark vacancy in the faces of some, and they wanted this vacancy filled with cruelty, with pain and with the sound of someone crying out. Only something vicious would satisfy them now, once they had been given permission to want it. They had changed from being a crowd doing what they were told to being a mob in search of some vast satisfaction that could come only with shrieks of pain and torn flesh and broken bones.

As time passed and we stood there waiting, I noticed this hunger spread like contagion until I believed that it had reached every single person there just as blood pumped from the heart makes its way inexorably to every part of the body.

When Pilate came out again, they listened but what he said made no difference.

"I find in him no fault at all," he said. "But ye had a custom that I should release unto you one prisoner at the Passover, will ye therefore that I release unto you, the King of the Jews?"

The crowd was ready. They replied "Not this man, but Barabbas!" And Barabbas the thief then appeared and he was set free to roars of approval from the crowd. And then there was a shout from somewhere and people at the front appeared to be able to see something that we could not see and there was confusion among the crowd and a sort of impatience as well, with people piling into the square so that we were no longer standing to the side but closer to the centre, all three of us staying together, saying nothing, making every effort not to be noticed. Everyone's full attention was on the balcony; they knew what was shortly to appear and were merely waiting for this great satisfaction.

And then it came and there was a gasp from the crowd, it was a gasp of delight before it was anything but it also contained shock and a sort of unease that grew into a hunger for more and thus the gasping became cheering and yelling and cat-calling because on the balcony with blood streaming down

his face and a thing made of thorns pushed back into the side
of his head, my son came wearing the purple robe of a king,
which seemed to hang on his shoulders in a way that made me
understand that his hands were tied behind his back. There
were soldiers all around him. The crowd began to laugh and
roar as the soldiers pushed him around on the balcony. I could
sense from the way he responded to being pushed that something had happened to weaken him. He seemed beaten down,
almost resigned. As soon as Pilate spoke again, the crowd began
to interrupt him, but he demanded that he be heard.

"Behold this man!" he said.

At the front and, I noticed, all around the edges of the
crowd, the chief priests began to lead the people in shouting
"Crucify him, crucify him." Pilate once more demanded silence.
He moved closer to my son to hold him steady and prevent the
soldiers from pushing him. He shouted to the chief priest "Take
ye him and crucify him, for I find no fault in him." And one
of the chief priests shouted "We have a law, and by our law he
ought to die, because he calls himself the Son of God!" Once
more Pilate withdrew and ordered the prisoner to be taken
back with him. I noticed as he turned—and I could see his face
clearly—that he looked at the crowd with fear and puzzlement.
Although it seemed at this point that Pilate was considering
the idea of releasing him, I realize now that I was alone in letting that hope linger. Everyone else knew that something was
being played out for the sake of the future, that nothing mattered now except the killing. So when they returned again and
Pilate shouted "Behold your king!" it did nothing but enrage
the crowd. All around they shouted the words "Away with him,
away with him, crucify him," as though these words if put into

action would mean infinite joy and pleasure, a sense of plenty and fulfillment. When Pilate roared again "Shall I crucify your king?" it was only as you would throw a stick to a dog. It was a game they seemed to be playing as they answered "We have no king but Caesar." Then he was delivered by Pilate to the crowd and the crowd was fully prepared; each one of them would have personally helped to organize the suffering had they been called upon. We edged slowly and with difficulty to the side so that we were ahead of a group which had formed, with men yelping and shouting greetings to their friends, and a sense that everybody's blood was filled with venom, a venom which came in the guise of energy, activity, shouting, laughing, roaring instructions as they paved the way for a grim procession to a hill beyond.

As we pushed our way to the front and tried to make sure that we were not separated from one another, each of us in our own way must have looked like the rest of those present, it must have seemed that we too were hungry with excitement at a glorious duty being performed, that someone who claimed to be king should be mocked and paraded and fully humiliated before being put to a painful death on a hill so that all could see him as he died. And it was strange too that the fact that my shoes hurt me, that they were not made for this bustle and this heat, preyed on my mind sometimes as a distraction from what was really happening.

I gasped when I saw the cross. They had it ready, waiting for him. It was too heavy to be carried and so they made him drag it through the crowd. I noticed how he tried to remove the thorns from around his head a number of times, but the efforts did not succeed and seemed instead to make them further push themselves into the skin and into the bone of his skull and his forehead. Each time he lifted his hands to see if he could ease the pain of this, some men behind him grew impatient and they came with clubs and whips to press him forward. For a time he seemed to forget all pain and he pushed the cross forward or pulled it. We moved quickly ahead of him. I still wondered if his followers had a plan, if they were waiting, or were disguised among the crowd as we were. I did not want to ask and it would have been impossible now anyway, and I was alert that any word we said or look we gave in the frenzy of things could have made us, any one of us, a victim too, to be kicked, or stoned, or taken away.

It was when I caught his eye that things changed. We had moved ahead and suddenly I turned and I saw that once again he was trying to remove the thorns that were cutting into his forehead and the back of his head and, failing to do anything to help himself, he lifted his head for a moment and his eyes caught mine. All of the worry, all of the shock, seemed to focus on a point in my chest. I cried out and made to run towards him but was held back by my companions, Mary whispering to me that I would have to be quiet and controlled or I would be recognized and taken away.

He was the boy I had given birth to and he was more defenceless now than he had been then. And in those days after he was born, when I held him and watched him, my thoughts included the thought that I would have someone now to watch over me when I was dying, to look after my body when I had died. In those days if I had even dreamed that I would see him bloody, and the crowd around filled with zeal that he should be bloodied more, I would have cried out as I cried out that day and the cry would have come from a part of me that is the core of me. The rest of me is merely flesh and blood and bone.

With Mary and our guide constantly telling me that I must not attempt to speak to him, that I must not cry out again, I followed them towards the hill. It was easy to fit in with those who were there, everyone talking or laughing, some leading horses or donkeys, others eating and drinking, the soldiers shouting in a language we did not understand, some of them with red hair and broken teeth and coarse faces. It was like a marketplace, but more intense somehow, as the act that was about to take place was going to make a profit for both seller and buyer. All the time I felt it would still be easy for someone to slip away unnoticed and I had a hope that his supporters might have planned a way for him to escape through this throng and out of the city to somewhere safe. But then, at the top of the hill, I saw some of them digging a hole and I realized that the people here meant business, they were here for one reason only, even though it might look like a gathering of motley groups.

We waited and it took an hour or maybe more for procession to arrive. It became easy somehow to tell the difference between those who were there for a reason, who were in the pay of somebody, acting on instructions, and those who were merely there as spectators. What was strange was how little attention some of them paid as others set about nailing him to the cross and, then, using ropes, trying to pull the cross towards the hole they had dug and balance it there.

For the nailing part, we stood back. Each of the nails was longer than my hand. Five or six of the men had to hold him and stretch out his arm along the cross and then, as they started to drive the first nail into him, at the point where the wrist meets the hand, he howled with pain and resisted them as jets of blood spurted out and the hammering began as they sought to get the long spike of the nail into the wood, crushing his hand and his arm against the cross as he writhed and roared out. When it was done, he did everything to stop them stretching out his other arm. One of them held his shoulder and one the upper arm, but still he managed to hold his arm in against his chest so they had to call for help. And then they held him and drove in a second nail so that his two arms were outstretched on the wood.

I tried to see his face as he screamed in pain, but it was so contorted in agony and covered in blood that I saw no one I recognized. It was the voice I recognized, the sounds he made that belonged only to him. I stood and looked around. There were other things going on—horses being shoed and fed, games being played, insults and jokes being hurled, and fires lit to cook food, with the smoke rising and blowing all around the hill. It seems hard to fathom now that I stayed there and watched this, that I did not run towards him, or call out to him. But I did not. I watched in horror, but I did not move or make a sound. Nothing would have worked against the quality of their determination. Nothing would have worked against how prepared they were, and fast-moving. But it seems odd, none-theless, that we could have watched, that I could have made a decision not to put myself in danger. We watched because we had no choice. I did not cry out or run to rescue him because it would have made no difference. I would have been cast aside like something blown in on the wind. But what is also strange, what seems strange after all these years, is that I had the capacity then to control myself, to weigh things up, to watch and do nothing and know that that was right. We held each other and stood back. That is what we did. We held each other and stood back as he howled out words that I could not catch. And maybe I should have moved towards him then, no matter what the consequences would have been. It would not have mattered, but at least I would not have to go over and over it now, wondering how I could not have run towards them and pulled them back and shouted out words, how I could have watched and remained still and silent. But that is what I did.

When I could, I asked our guardian how long it would take for him to die and was told that because of the nails and the amount of blood he seemed to have lost and the heat of the sun then it could be quick, but it could still take a day unless they came and broke his legs and then it would be quicker. There was a man in charge, I was told, and he knew how to make the time go faster or slow it down, he was an expert, that is what he did in the same way as others were experts in crops and seasons, the time to harvest the fruit from the trees, or the time it took a child to come into the world. They could make sure, I was told, that no more blood would be spilled, or they could even turn the cross away from the sun, or they could use spears to pierce his flesh, and this would mean that he would die within hours, before nightfall. This would mean that he would die before the Sabbath, but for this, I was told, permission would have to be given by the Romans, by Pilate himself. And if Pilate could not be found, then there were always men among the crowd who could stand in for Pilate and give permission. I almost wanted to ask if there was still time to save him, if he could be rescued and still live, but, in reality, I knew that it was too late for that. I had seen the nails before they went into the space between his wrists and his hands.

Then I saw that other crosses were being raised with men tied to them with ropes, but the wood seemed to be too heavy, or the crosses had been badly made, and each time they had them standing the crosses would slip over and fall back to the ground.

I was watching anything, a cloud billowing across the sky, a stone, a man standing in front of me, anything to distract me from the moans that came from close by. I asked myself if there was anything I could do to pretend that this was not happening, that it had happened in the past to someone else, or that it was going on in a future I would never have to live through. Because I had been watching with such care, I could tell that a group of men, some Romans, some Elders, stood by the side, and they had horses, and it was how they observed the scene and circled around each other that made me realize that they were the ones in control, that many other events here were random, part of the day before the Sabbath, but these men seemed gruff, determined, well-fed, serious. Suddenly, I saw that among them was my cousin Marcus and that he had seen me. Before the others could stop me I ran towards him and I knew how foolish I must have seemed, how helpless and poor and shrill. I suppose I had my arms out and I suppose my face was wet with tears and I suppose I made no sense. I remember the looks of indifference or mild exasperation from some of the other men being mirrored in Marcus's face and then changing into a dark brutality as he told me to get away from them. I know I did not use his name. I know I did not say that he was my cousin. And

I saw fear in his face and then I saw how quickly it faded and it changed into a determination that I would be removed from the orbit of these men whom no one else had dared approach. He nodded to someone and it was that man, who later played dice close to the hanging bodies, who became the one who watched me all the time, who seemed to know who I was and who, I believe, had instructions to hold me, capture me, once the death had taken place and the crowd had dispersed. Later, I realized that they all believed that we would wait until the end to take the body and bury it. It was one thing the Romans had learned about us; we would not leave a corpse to the elements. We would wait, no matter what the danger.

My guardian, who comes now to this house, and the other one whom I like even less, they want my description of these hours to be simple, they want to know what words I heard, they want to know about my grief only if it comes as the word "grief," or the word "sorrow." Even though one of them witnessed what I witnessed, he does not want it registered as confusion, with strange memories of the sky darkening and brightening again, or of other voices shouting down the moans and cries and whimpers, and even the silence that came from the figure on the cross. And the smoke from fires that grew more acrid and stung all our eyes as no wind seemed to blow in any direction. They do not want to know how one of the other crosses keeled over regularly and had to be propped up, nor do they want to know about the man who came and fed rabbits to a savage and indignant bird in a cage too small for its wing-span.

As many things happened in those hours as there are seconds. I moved from feeling that I could do something to realizing that I could not. I moved from being distracted by the coldest thoughts, thoughts that if this was not happening to me, since I was not the one being crucified to death, then it could not really be happening at all. Thoughts of him as a baby, as a part of my flesh, his heart having grown from my heart. And of running to the others to be held or ask questions. Or watching the men in case any of them made a sign that this should end more quickly. Or coming to understand that the reason Marcus had enticed me to the city and given me an address was so that I could be held when it was over, or indeed the day before.

And then in the last hour, as the crowd thinned out, and some of the men made their way down the hill, there was no time for wondering, or realizing, or thinking. No time for looking around or finding ways to be distracted. In this last hour, the anguish of hanging in the sun with nails in your hands and feet seemed to grow more intense, came in fierce shrieks and then gasps. And all of us waited, all of us knew that the end was coming and all of us watched his face, his body, unsure if he knew we were there with him until close to the end when he seemed to open his eyes and tried to speak but none of us could catch his words, which came with too much effort for anyone to hear. They were ways of letting us know that he was alive, and, strangely, despite the pain he suffered, despite this vast public display of his defeat and the fact that I had all the time desperately wanted it to be over quickly, I did not want it to be over now.

As it neared the end, our guardian, his follower, the one

who comes here, who pays my bills and orders my affairs, told me that we would have to leave quickly once he died, that others would come to look after the washing of his body and burial, that there was a path at the back of the hill and if we were prepared to go towards it in ones, then he could ensure our escape, but even if we escaped, he said, someone would follow us, or come looking for us, so we would have to make our way through the night on foot by the light of the moon and the stars and hide each day where we could. I looked at him as he spoke and I saw something that I see still in him now—no grief, no sorrow, no fuss, something cold, as though life is a business to be managed, that our time on earth requires planning and regulation and careful foresight.

"He is not dead yet," I said to him. "He is not dead yet. I will stay with him until he dies."

For a moment I glanced over towards the men at the side. I noticed that Marcus was missing and the man who had been following me was missing too. For a second, puzzled, I looked behind me to see if they were leaving or had joined some other gathering. I saw them then, both of them, and they were with the man who had been at the wedding in Cana, the strangler, and they were pointing towards me and Mary and our guardian, singling us out among the crowd. The strangler was watching and nodding calmly as each one of us was identified. Later, as the years went by, I would say to myself that the decision I made then was for Mary's sake, that I realized that I had led her here and that now I was to be the cause of her being strangled. I remember what Marcus had told me, the man could do it without making a sound or leaving a mark. But it was not the possibility of Mary's death by silent strangling, the image of her body writhing and resisting as his thumbs pushed in on her neck to break it, that caused me to run towards our guardian and to tell him that we must go now, go as he had said, stealthily in ones and then move fast, travel through the night to wherever we might be safe. It was my own safety I thought of, it was to protect myself. I was suddenly afraid, and more afraid now that the danger had edged towards me, than I had been all those hours.

It is only now that I can admit this, only now that I can allow myself to say it. For years I have comforted myself with the thought of how long I remained there, how much I suffered then. But I must say it once, I must let the words out, that despite the panic, despite the desperation, the shrieking, despite the fact that his heart and his flesh had come from my heart and my flesh, despite the pain I felt, a pain that has never lifted, and will go with me into the grave, despite all of this, the pain was his and not mine. And when the possibility of being dragged away and choked arose, my first instinct was to flee and it was also my last instinct. In those hours I was powerless, but, nonetheless, I went from grief to further grief, wringing my hands, holding the others, watching with horror, I now knew what I would do. As our guardian said, I would leave others to wash his body and hold him and bury him when his death came. I would leave him to die alone if I had to. And that is what I did. Once I signalled my agreement, Mary slipped away first and we watched her go out of the side of our eyes. I did not look at the figure on the cross again. Perhaps I had looked enough. Perhaps I was right to save myself when I could. But it does not feel like that now and it never has. But I will say it now because it has to be said by someone once: I did it to save myself. I did it for no other reason. I watched our guardian slip away and I pretended not to notice. I moved towards the cross as if I was going to sit at the foot of it and wring my hands as I waited for his final moments. And then I slipped around the back. I pretended I was searching for something or someone, or a place to relieve myself where I could not be easily seen. And then I followed our guardian and Mary down the hill on the other side, walking slowly, walking slowly away.

I have dreamed I was there. I have dreamed that I held my broken son in my arms when he was all bloody and then again when he was washed, that I had him back for that time, that I touched his flesh and put my hands on his face, which had grown beautiful and gaunt now that his suffering was over. I touched his feet and his hands where the nails had been. I pulled the thorns out of his head and washed the blood out of his hair. They left me with him, the others, Mary and the guardian but the others too who had come to be with him at the end, who had put themselves in danger to declare their belief in him. And we were left there with him. Since the grisly vicious job had been done and a man had been made to die splayed out against the sky on a hill so the world would know and see and remember, those who had made him die had no more reason to remain. They were eating and drinking some-where, or waiting to be paid. Thus the busy hill, so filled not long before with smoke and shouting, with cruelty and hard faces, now became a soft place for weeping. We held him and touched him, he who was both heavy and weightless, the blood all gone from his body, his body like marble or ivory in its rich paleness. His body was growing stiff and lifeless but some other part of him, what he had given us in those last hours, what had come from his suffering, remained in the air around us like something sweet to comfort us.

I have dreamed this. And there are times when I have let the dream into the day to live with me, when I have sat in that chair and felt that I was holding him, his body all cleansed of pain and myself cleansed too of the pain that I felt, which was part of his pain, the pain we shared. All of this is easy to imagine. It is what really happened that is unimaginable, and it is what really happened that I must face now in these months before I go into my grave or else everything that happened will become a sweet story that will grow poisonous as bright berries that hang low on trees. I do not know why it matters that I should tell the truth to myself at night, why it should matter that the truth should be spoken at least once in the world. Because the world is a place of silence, the sky at night when the birds have gone is a vast silent place. No words will make the slightest difference to the sky at night. They will not brighten it or make it less strange. And the day too has its own deep indifference to anything that is said.

I tell the truth not because it will change night into day or make the days endless in their beauty and the comfort they offer us, we who are old. I speak simply because I can, because enough has happened and because the chance might not come again. It will not be long maybe when I begin again to dream that I waited on the hill that day and held him naked in my arms, it will not be long before that dream, so close to me now and so real, will fill the air and will make its way backwards into time and thus become what happened, or what must have happened, what happened, what I know happened, what I saw happened.

What happened was this. They held me between them as they ran and it became clear to me that our guardian did not have anything planned. He knew as little as we did about where he was going. We could not go back into the city. He had some money, but we had no food. It struck me that he was urging us forward so he could save himself, that the grand plan for my protection came later, or was there too maybe, but it was not dominant in those hours. In the way they work now, my guests who come, they try to make connections, weave a pattern, a meaning into things, and they ask me to help, and I will help them as I have done already, but not now. Now I know how random it was and uncertain, and there are things that happened on that journey that I do not care even now to conjure up. I know we were not good in those days because we were desperate. We took clothes because we needed clothes and I took shoes because I needed shoes. We did not take money and we did not kill anyone. I don't believe we killed anyone but there were things I did not see. We moved as quickly as we could and sometimes there was no food and sometimes we were sure we were being followed or had been noticed. We told whoever we needed to tell that this was my daughter with her husband and we were travelling without any goods or donkeys to carry us because my son had gone ahead in a caravan with all our belongings. Those lies do not matter, maybe even other things we did to help us on our journey do not matter, but I cannot be sure.

What is hard to understand is that our dreams matter. Just as we made progress by night more than by day after what happened on that hill, at least for those first days, so too what came when we were asleep lingers more pressingly within me now than it did then. It is strange that it does not seem to matter now that we terrorized a household which lay alone, vulnerable and innocent, in the countryside, and that we took food and clothes and shoes and three donkeys which we let loose after a few hours, and that our guardian tied a man and his wife and their children up, having threatened them, so that they could not follow us. We saw that. I wore the shoes and the clothes and we made better progress using their donkeys. All of that happened.

But what happened also was the dream we had; Mary and I shared a dream. I did not know you could share a dream. In the years when I was married we dreamed separate dreams, although we lay close beside each other, often touching each other through the night. Dreams belong to each of us alone, just as pain does. Now in these desperate days when we were starving sometimes and out of breath and filled with fear and when Mary and I realized that our guardian had no plan, he was taking us towards water, or the sea, he was depending on luck, and that as each day went by, unless we found a ship or shelter, and the chances of our not being captured were growing dim, Mary and I remained close. We held each other as we walked; we slept in each other's arms for warmth and protection. And both of us knew that if we were caught we would be murdered, stoned to death, or strangled, and left to rot. We barely spoke to our guardian and barely managed to conceal our contempt for him, so great was our fear of being captured now after all of this, so great was our rage at being lured into the wilds by a man who was incompetent, with all the trappings of pomposity around him dying away through lack of food and pure exhaustion.

We both dreamed that my son came back to life. We both dreamed we were sleeping and there was a well made of wood and stone, a well that was much used because it went deep into the earth and yielded a sweeter, cooler, clearer water than other wells. We were alone there. It was the morning, but no one yet had come to the well as the sun had just risen. We both slept leaning against the stone. In front of us there was no pathway, which was strange. There were some olive trees in the distance, but none close, and no sound, no birdsong, or bleating from goats, nothing. Both of us sleeping, still in our robes, and the dawn light. No sign that our guardian was anywhere close, and the fear and the manic movement of the days quite absent. And suddenly both of us were woken by the sound of water gurgling up from the earth as if someone invisible had come to fetch water and the water was rising as though unbidden and then spilling over. I am sure that the water spilled over and that I was fully awoken now by it as it wet my robe. But still I did not stand up; instead I put my hand into the water to make sure that it was real, and it was. But Mary stood up to avoid the water and what she saw made her gasp. I looked at her, but I did not see what she saw at first because I was so surprised by the water, which now seemed to be rushing out of the well, it was pumping out in vast spurts and spilling over and trickling down towards the trees, gradually forming a small stream.

And then I turned and I saw him, he had come back to us, he was rising with the water, its power pushing him up from the earth. He was naked and the places where he had been wounded, including his hands, his feet, his legs where the bones had been broken, his forehead where the thorns had been, had blue marks around them and were open and gaping. The rest of his body was white. Mary held him as the water delivered him from the well and she placed him across my lap. We both touched him. It was a whiteness that we both noticed, a whiteness that is hard to describe. Both of us remarked on its purity and smooth, luminous beauty.

In our dream there were moments before we woke in which he opened his eyes, in which he moved his hands and then his arms, and groaned almost, but it was gentle, both the movement and the sound. He seemed to have neither pain nor any memory of what he had been through. But the marks were there on his body. We did not speak to him. We simply held him and he seemed to be alive.

And then he was still, or he was dead, or I woke, or we both woke. And there was nothing else. Because we could not contain ourselves, our guide heard every word. Something changed in him then, he began to smile and said that he had always known that this would happen, that it was part of what had been foretold. He made us recount it in detail and when we had done so a number of times and he seemed to have committed it to memory, he said we were safe, that something else would happen which would guide us towards wherever it was we needed to go. There was a lightness in us then, a lightness caused by hunger and maybe by fear. Whatever it was it left us free.

I knew and Mary knew that we were moving blindly and I realized at certain times that we would be safer were Mary to separate from us and make her way home. Later, when a house was found for us, we could discuss this more calmly. We both knew that I could never go home, that I could never appear in any of the places where I would be known. But she could and

I knew she wanted to. And then the calm days ended. The end was caused by food and by rest and by the change in our guide, which gave him a sort of glow. This glow meant that one or two people, complete strangers, and then others who knew he had been a follower, offered to help him. Through them he could send for help; and then he could tell us that we would soon be safe, that a boat would come for us and take us to Ephesus where there was a house waiting, a house where we would always be protected. He did not understand that his reassurances, that the comforts he offered us, seemed to make no difference to the grief that came now, the shock and the shame at what we had done. We had left others to bury my son, or perhaps he had not been buried at all. We had run to a place where what happened in our dreams took on more flesh, had more substance, than our lives when we were conscious, alert, aware. And that seemed right for some days and maybe both of us hoped that the future would be coated in dreams too; and then it collapsed, all of it, and I knew that Mary would want to go, that she no longer wanted to be with me. I knew what would happen and it did: one morning she simply was not there in the other bed when I woke. And our guide had arranged for her to go since she wanted to. It was not a time when farewells were necessary or would have made any difference. I did not mind the method of her going. But I was alone with him now and I was going to have to work out a way of handling him. I also needed to make distinctions which were clear. From then on I wanted dreams to have their place, to let them belong to the night. And I wanted what happened, what I saw, what I did, to belong to the day. Until I died I hoped that I would live in full recognition of the difference between the two. I hope I have done that.

*   *   *

It is day now and what comes in here to this room is called light. What was strange as we boarded the vessel that took me here and sailed through storms and calm seas was that I had developed a hunger for catastrophe, that as we boarded I desperately needed, as though for my peace of mind, our guide or one of our helpers to fall into the water and howl for help and disappear and rise again and then be found later floating away dead. I wanted it back, whatever it was. I saw it not as itself, but as image, or simple reminder. When I saw a man, I saw a violent death, and I felt I would be ready now to witness it, as an animal who has been in the wild will know what to expect, or what to do, when a gentle hand comes with food presuming the animal is tame. I had been made wild by what I saw and nothing has ever changed that. I have been unhinged by what I saw in daylight and no darkness will assuage that, or lessen what it did to me.

I do not often leave the house. I am careful and watchful; now that the days are shorter and the nights are cold, when I look out of the windows I have begun to notice something that surprises me and holds me. There is a richness in the light. It is as if, in becoming scarce, in knowing that it has less time to spread its gold over where we are, it lets loose something more intense, something that is filled with a shivering clarity. And then when it begins to fade, it seems to leave raked shadows on everything. And during that hour, the hour of ambiguous light, I feel safe to slip out and breathe the dense air when the colours are fading and the sky seems to be pulling them in, calling them home, until gradually nothing stands out in the

73

landscape. It pleases me and makes me feel almost invisible as I walk towards the Temple to spend a few minutes standing close to one of the pillars watching the shadows deepen and all things preparing for the night.

I move like a cat as I stand and edge forward and then stand again. Even though I feel that I cannot be seen or noticed as easily as I might were it noon or morning, I am always alert, as one of those thin wild cats is alert, ready to dart away with speed at the slightest hint of danger.

On one of those days I realized that I had stayed too long in the temple and that night was already falling when I came out into the clearing. I knew that I would have to move with speed to be home before darkness came as the nights were nights of pure blackness with hardly a sliver of a moon whose light would be too faint to guide me. I could not therefore use the winding path I always used, but make my way more directly, climbing as best I could the short, steep slope that would lead me home in better time.

And then, in the fading light in this place where I have come to end my days, I passed stones that I had not seen before. Slabs of thin stone, like teeth, jutting up from the earth as though they grew there. I felt free to lean on one of them when my hip hurt from walking too fast. And then something in the grass and scrub, some animal sound, caused me to turn and I was so frightened by what I saw that I almost ran. Carved into the stone were two figures almost as tall as I am, and on both of them shone the last slanting rays of the sun, hitting the whiteness of the stone and making it glisten. One of the figures was young and almost naked. The expression on his face was placid, innocent. I felt that he could easily have stepped out from where he had been carved and come towards me, as the light seemed to intensify. Despite my initial alarm, I was not now afraid of him. Beside him stood an older man with a beard and his hand was to his face and it was clear that he was weeping, that he too lived in loss. He was in distress; something had happened of which the young man seemed unaware. Maybe that is how the dead are, they are unaware, they do not the miss the world or know what happens here. As I stood and watched both men, the young one I imagined to be dead and his father alive and filled with the anguish of those of us who are in the world still, I noticed under the young man, lying crouched, was a child who was crying, who seemed curled up in grief wilder than the grief of the standing man. Then as the rays of the sun lowered, I saw in the lingering light that all around me were stones with carvings, with figures, even animals, and also some words. In the distance they had seemed random, things that had just been left there, but now it was clear that they had been put here for a purpose, and the carvings must mean something, and as I walked away from them quickly I knew that they stood for death.

There are times in these days before death comes with my name in whispers, calling me towards darkness, lulling me towards rest, when I know that I want more from the world. Not much, but more. It is simple. If water can be changed into wine and the dead can be brought back, then I want time pushed back. I want to live again before my son's death happened, or before he left home, when he was a baby and his father was alive and there was ease in the world. I want one of those golden Sabbath days, days without wind when there were prayers on our lips, when I joined the women and intoned the words, the supplication to God to give justice to the weak and the orphan, maintain the right of the lowly and the destitute, rescue the needy, deliver them from the hands of the wicked. When I said these words to God, it mattered that my husband and son were close by and that soon, when I had walked home alone and sat in the shadows with my hands joined, I would hear their footsteps returning and I would await my son's shy smile as the door was opened for him by his father and then we would sit in silence waiting for the sun to disappear when we could talk again and eat together and prepare with ease for the peaceful night after the day when we had renewed ourselves, when our love for each other, for God and the world, had deepened and spread.

This is over now. The boy became a man and left home and became a dying figure hanging on a cross. I want to be able to imagine that what happened to him will not come, it will see us and decide—not now, not them. And we will be left in peace to grow old.

They will return, my minders, my guards. They have me watched in any case. In a few days they will know that I woke in the dawn like this and stood in this room. Somebody will have seen a shadow, something through the window, or heard a sound. I am not alone here. Perhaps they pay Farina to watch me and report on me, or threaten her with something if she does not. Or it could be one of the others whom I pass and do not speak to. It does not matter.

And each time we start again at the beginning and each time they move from being excited by a detail to being exasperated by something that comes soon afterwards, another detail maybe, a refusal to add what they want me to add, or an opinion I express on their tone or their efforts to make simple sense of things which are not simple.

But maybe they are simple. Maybe when I die, and I will die soon, they will be even simpler. It will be as though what I saw and felt did not happen, or happened in the same way a small flap of a bird's wing in the high sky happens on a day when there is no wind. They want to make what happened live for ever, they told me. What is being written down, they say, will change the world.

"The world?" I asked. "All of it?"

"Yes," the man who had been my guide said, "all of it."

I must have looked perplexed.

"She does not understand," he said to his companion, and it was true. I did not understand.

"He was indeed the Son of God," he said.

And then, patiently, he began to explain to me what had happened to me at my son's conception as the other nodded and encouraged him. I barely listened. I had other things to do. I know what happened. I know that my own happiness in those first months when I was with child felt strange and special, that I lived in a way that was different, that I often stood at the window and looked at the light outside and felt that the new life within me, the second heart beating, fulfilled me beyond anything I had ever imagined. Later, I learned that this is how we all prepare ourselves to give birth and to nurture, that it comes from the body itself and makes its way into the spirit and it does not seem ordinary. So I smiled when they spoke because they seemed to know something that was true about the light and grace that came at that time and for once I liked how eager and sure they were.

It was when they came to the last part that I stood up from the chair and moved away from them, assaulted by their words.

"He died to redeem the world," the other man said. "His death has freed mankind from darkness and from sin. His father sent him into the world that he might suffer on the cross."

"His father?" I asked. "His father . . . ?"

"His suffering was necessary," he interrupted, "it was how mankind would be saved."

"Saved?" I asked and raised my voice. "Who has been saved?"

"Those who came before him and those who live now and those who are not yet born," he said.

"Saved from death?" I asked.

"Saved for eternal life," he said. "Everyone in the world will know eternal life."

"Oh, eternal life!" I replied. "Oh, everyone in the world!"

I looked at both of them, their eyes hooded and something appearing dark in their faces.

"Is that what it was for?"

They caught one another's eye and for the first time I felt the enormity of their ambition and the innocence of their belief.

"Who else knows this?"

"It will be known," one of them said.

"Through your words?" I asked.

"Through our words and the words of others of his disciples."

"You mean," I asked, "the men who followed him?"

"Yes."

"Are they still alive?"

"Yes."

"They were hiding when he died," I said. "They were hiding when he died."

"They were there when he rose again," one of them said.

"They saw his grave," I said. "I never saw his grave, I never washed his body."

"You were there," my guide said. "You held his body when it was taken down from the cross."

His companion nodded.

"You watched us as we covered his body in spices and wound his body in linen cloths and buried him in a sepulchre near the place where he was crucified. But you were not with us, you were in a place where you were protected when he came among us three days after his death and spoke to us before he rose to be with his father."

"His father," I said.

"He was the Son of God," the man said, "and he was sent by his father to redeem the world."

"By his death, he gave us life," the other said. "By his death, he redeemed the world."

I turned towards them then and whatever it was in the expression on my face, the rage against them, the grief, the fear, they both looked up at me alarmed and one of them began to move towards me to stop me saying what it was I now wanted to say. I edged back from them and stood in the corner. I whispered it at first and then I said it louder and as he moved away from me and almost cowered in the corner I whispered it again, slowly, carefully, giving it all my breath, all my life, the little that is left in me.

"I was there," I said. "I fled before it was over but if you want witnesses then I am one and I can tell you now, when you say that he redeemed the world, I will say that it was not worth it. It was not worth it."

They departed that night on a caravanserai, which was making its way towards the islands and there was in their tone and manner a new distance from me, something close to fear but maybe even closer to pure exasperation and disgust. But they left me money and provisions and they left me a sense that I was still under their protection. It was easy to be polite to them. They are not fools. I admire how deliberate they are, how exact their plans, how dedicated they are, how different from the group of unshaven brutes and twitchers, men who could not look at women, who came to my house after my husband's death and sat with my son, talking nonsense through the night. They will thrive and prevail and I will die.

I do not go to the Synagogue now. All of that is gone. I would be noticed; my strangeness would stand out. But I go with Farina to the other Temple and sometimes I go alone in the morning when I wake or later when there are shadows coming over the world, presaging night. I move quietly. I speak to her in whispers, the great goddess Artemis, bountiful with her arms outstretched and her many breasts waiting to nurture those who come towards her. I tell her how much I long now to sleep in the dry earth, to go to dust peacefully with my eyes shut in a place near here where there are trees. In the meantime, when I wake in the night, I want more. I want what happened not to have happened, to have taken another course. How easily it might not have happened! How easily we could have been spared! It would not have taken much. Even the thought of its possibility comes into my body now like a new freedom. It lifts the darkness and pushes away the grief. It is as if a traveller, weary after days of walking in a dry desert, a place void of shade, were to come to a hilltop and see below a city, an opal set in emerald, filled with plenty, a city filled with wells and trees, a marketplace laden with fish and fowl and the fruits of the earth, a place redolent with the smell of cooking and spices.

I begin to walk down towards it along a soft path. I am being led into this strange place of souls, along great narrow bridges spanning gurgling, steaming water, like lava in the dying glow, with island meadows filled with vital growth below. Being led by no one. All around there is silence and soothing, dwindling light. The world has loosened, like a woman preparing for bed who lets her hair flow free. And I am whispering the words, knowing that words matter, and smiling as I say them to the shadows of the gods of this place who linger in the air to watch me and hear me.